Dec 1 95

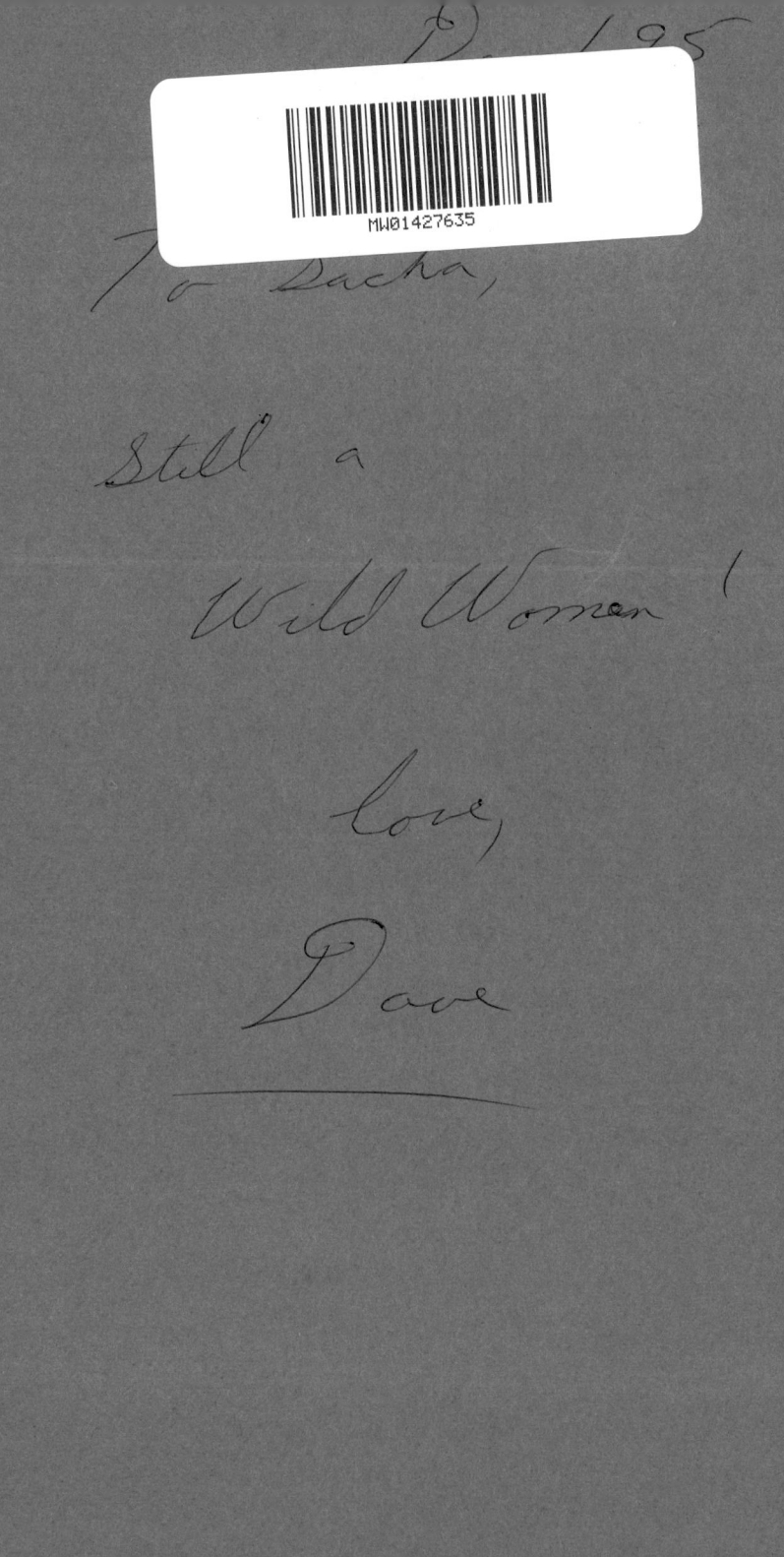

To Sacha,

Still a

Wild Woman!

love,

Dave

SMALL SOULS UNDER SIEGE

SMALL SOULS UNDER SIEGE

by
Anne Dandurand

translated by
Robert Majzels

CORMORANT BOOKS

Petites âmes sous ultimatum copyright © Anne Dandurand, 1991
Translation copyright © Robert Majzels, 1995
Translation assisted by the Canada Council.
This translation was approved by the author.

from *Petites âmes sous ultimatum*,
Montreal, XYZ, 1991

The publisher wishes to acknowledge the generous assistance of the Canada Council, the Ontario Arts Council, and the Ontario Publishing Centre.

The French version of "Celebration of Good Works" was published separately, in an earlier version, in the anthology *Saignant ou beurre noir?* (L'instant même, Québec, 1992).

"La dernière journée du milk-shake" was awarded the grand prize for short fiction by the Salon du Livre de la Jeunesse (Paris, 1989) and was a finalist in the Radio-Canada short fiction contest 1989–1990.

Edited by Gena K. Gorrell.

Cover from a silkscreen by Roy Bishop, *Images II*, courtesy of the artist, from the collection of the Canada Council Art Bank.

Cover design by Artcetera Graphics, Dunvegan, Ontario.

Author photograph © Josée Lambert photographe.

Printed and bound in Canada.

Published by Cormorant Books Inc.,
RR 1, Dunvegan, Ontario, Canada K0C 1J0

No part of this publication may be reproduced, stored in a retrieval system or transmitted, except for purposes of review, without the prior written permission of the publisher or, in the case of photocopying or other reprographic copying, a licence from:
CANCOPY (Canadian Copyright Licensing Agency),
6 Adelaide Street East, Suite 900, Toronto, Ontario, M5C 1H6.

CANADIAN CATALOGUING IN PUBLICATION DATA

Dandurand, Anne, 1953-
[Petites âmes sous ultimatum. English]
     Small souls under siege

Short stories.
Translation of: Petites âmes sous ultimatum.
ISBN 0-920953-81-6

     I. Title. II. Title: Petites âmes sous ultimatum. English.
PS8557.A52P4813 1995   C843'.54   C95-900180-8
PQ3919.2.D247P4813 1995

The wind is rising!... We must try to live!
Paul Valéry, *Charmes*

CONTENTS

SHIELDED BY A COMMA 9

MISUNDERSTANDING IN SVENDBORG 19

BODY OF SEASONS 25

THE INSEMINATION OF THE SKY 35

A THOUSAND AND ONE MINOTAURS 41

THE POSSESSION OF JACQUES BRAISE 55

COURAGE MAKES A FINE DAGGER 67

THE LAST DAY FOR MILKSHAKES 79

CELEBRATION OF GOOD WORKS 91

IN THE WARMTH OF A PHRASE 99

SHIELDED BY A COMMA

Though grief and perhaps even mourning may be waiting here at home for her, still I long for J.'s return, although I completely understand why, once or twice a year, she has to go and shake her foreign editors out of their relative apathy, I can picture her, so pale and thin, sitting in front of a massive oaken desk, smoking even more than usual, listening, as she has listened time and again for the last ten years, to the same old platitudes about the collapsing market and what a swamp the publishing industry is, and her sitting there with nothing in her pockets but the few humble arguments of her stubborn labour, wrenched from the silence of so many pre-dawn mornings, how I long for her return, she'll bring me postcards and photographs, she's always such a wreck when she comes back, misery flaunts itself far more insolently over there than it does here, I know it's her powerlessness that gets to her more than anything, she can never get over not being able to do something about all that suffering, I'll try to tell her, as I do each time, that I'm here, that she is after all taking care of me, which ought to count for something, I'll remind her of the very first time we met, it was an eleventh of January, sixteen years ago, I was only six, I was in my classroom, her mother was teaching me to speak and to read, not an easy task what with those retards and mongoloids constantly disrupting us, but J.'s mother had seen through to my intelligence, she knew my lack of intellectual and physical development was simply the result of my having been tied down to a hospital bed from birth, so J.'s mother taught me to speak and, more important, to read, because, though I was only six, until then the only thing I had ever wanted was to die, until then I had experienced nothing remotely like the joy of simply living, nothing but the infinite pain of living, in my child's mind I could not understand why those doctors had chosen to save me, a baby without an oesophagus, why not let me die, why go to all the trouble of manufacturing an artificial oesophagus, why put me through more than forty surgical operations in six years only to end up using a slice of my own small intestine to connect my throat and stomach, more or less, less actually, so that until J.'s mother taught me to read I had no reason to live, nothing but the pain of living, and then, that eleventh of January, J. came to see her mother in school, sixteen years ago she was thirty-five years old, she dressed all in black leather, with that shaggy head of hair and the sad charm of a woman no man loves, and the almost scary beauty of a woman who goes on using makeup in spite of everything, and much too much makeup at that, using eye shadow and lipstick as frail ramparts against solitude, J. approached my wheelchair and, softly, softly, asked me why I never stopped shaking my head, no one before J. had dealt with me so directly, before J. it had been nothing but looks full of pity or disgust, and suddenly for the first time I knew the meaning of dignity, because I could explain clearly, in my child's words, that as I'd been strapped to my hospital bed from birth to keep me from tearing my stitches or ripping out the intravenous tubes, my head was the only thing I could move, so that this head shaking had come to signify freedom and independence, as a matter of fact the habit has stuck, I shall be shaking my head for ever, as if to say no, no to medical experiments, no to the blindly cunning violence of the bureaucracy, no to all those tight-fisted hearts, I really wish J. would hurry up and come home, and when she gets here, to console her, I'll tell her the story of our first meeting, she'll claim she doesn't remember but that won't stop me, I'll remind her how my mama, exhausted from having already borne five children, and my papa, unemployed and alcoholic and so also exhausted, had abandoned me in one of those institutions supposedly for my own good, but not really for my good since I wasn't an idiot, just a child whose legs were too weak and who, since her birth, had been taught nothing except to listen, and who had to be forcefed, I've never enjoyed eating, my throat is always on fire, even the water and anti-rejection pills set my transplanted viscera ablaze, I'll probably never know the pleasure of passionate kisses that never want to end, in the Centre I would wheel myself around the library and read, at twelve I had the body of a five-year-old, and that's where, on the twenty-seventh of November, J. saw me for the second time, she had brought some children's books, review copies Lépervier had been sent through the mail, and then I have no idea how she managed it so that I could move in with her, she must have had to talk to the social services, what with me being classified as a "severe case" and her living alone, in a manner of speaking, in a second-floor apartment, inaccessible to the handicapped, but my J. is nothing if not hard-headed, what J. wants J. gets, something she never tires of repeating, always of course adding except with men, with men she can want all she likes, they never do, and has this become worse since I moved in, she denies it, claims it's her, she's too old now, too many shadows under her eyes, what made

13

her go and talk to the social services about taking me in, I like to think it's because I was reading in the library at the precise moment she came in, it was November and yet there was plenty of sunlight, and dust motes dancing in the rays, sunlight as though this might be the one day for a miracle, I was reading for the hundredth time the *Inhuman Hearts* volume of *The Thousand and One Nights*, the preceding and subsequent volumes being missing, but even torn and stained, *Inhuman Hearts* was the best thing in the library, and J. came straight for me, with her zany earrings, maybe too wild for someone forty-one years old, and she asked me if she could hold me in her arms, and as no one had ever taken me in their arms I suddenly found myself sobbing with relief, also drooling and snivelling, J. rocked me back and forth into numbness, swearing all the while that she would find a way to get me out of the Centre, and on June thirtieth of the following year she came to get me and I moved into her place, into the apartment she had managed to rent on a ground floor, she had ripped out all the doorsills so that my wheelchair could pass through, and installed handrails for me to grab hold of beside the bath and the toilet, and fixed up the light switches and door handles with wire and bits of wood so that I could open and shut them, and what's more, using the perforated strips from her printing paper, she had strung fine white garlands all across the ceilings, she offered me Lépervier's room, he claimed he didn't mind, he went to stay somewhere else, with one of his friends, Lépervier has no home, no bank account, nothing except for his dictionaries and a lousy computer, whenever J. is away he comes back to stay at our place to take care of me, the social services don't know about this, how could we trust them to understand that a penniless homosexual has the voice and, more, the kindness, of a guardian angel, still I wish J. would hurry back, on my seventeenth birthday she decorated my chair while I slept, with decals and fluorescent paint, you'd never know, to look at those long painted nails, how good J. is with her hands, how much she enjoys working with them, so that, thanks to her skulls and fire-spewing dragons, my wheelchair looked more like a Hell's Angels Harley Davidson, and the next day J. and I went out for a spin in the neighbourhood, the rustling of the trees in the park sounded like applause, and summer flooded our eyes with the bare-limbed beauty of young, carefree men, both of us were wearing sunglasses and we strolled a long time, and all our neighbours and the local merchants wished me happy birthday, especially the owner of the photocopy shop, who's been a paraplegic for the last twenty years, the result of an accident, and he faked a jealous fit over my gorgeous wheelchair, bawling that he had to have one just like it, afterwards J. and I even went for a drink, a beer for her, a crème de cacao for me, it's so much easier to swallow, we sat in the café on the corner of Duluth, which has an access ramp for wheelchairs, of course I was under age but the waiter pretended not to notice, and other starving artists like J. came in and joined us, a solo dancer with a head of wild hair, a playwright with a trembling look in her eye, a painter with pants covered in a baroque rainbow of splotches, we had so much fun all together, and later, back at home, J. promised me that as soon as one of her books made the bestseller list she would buy me a motorized wheelchair, so that I could roam around town to my heart's delight, so that I too could find a kind of independence, and that's how another dream entered the house, one more dream to store away with all the others in the phantoms' wardrobe, the one whose door opens all by itself at the strangest moments, but here the one dream we most often slip off its hanger is Lépervier's, for years J. and he have been imagining this great voyage in a motor-home across the three Americas, the two of them invading the Bronx or Bahía Blanca, going diving in the hot springs of Aguascalientes, when they're together J. and Lépervier have a way of concocting endless twilights, tides, horizons, but today he knows he won't be going anywhere ever again, not even out of this house, J. has got to get back soon, it used to be that when she went off on one of her trips Lépervier was the one who wheeled me through the streets, always after eleven at night he would wheel me through the streets, through the lashing gales of winter or the damp, jazzy heat-waves of summer, other times he would push me along by the river while he raved about or picked apart the book he happened to be reading that week, he too could never have faced life without his love of books, and then there were the times when his soul teetered on the edge of ruin, when he would start sobbing miserably in the empty street, but he always put an end to it by saying, pass me the teapot so I can drink down this tempest, and that would always make the two of us laugh because Lépervier has never been much of a tea drinker, nowadays he can't drink much of anything, he wheeled me through the streets, I'd light a Gitane for him, on the way from time to time we bumped into an acquaintance of his, night has a way of igniting strange fires in a look, whenever they enquired about his health Lépervier quickly changed the subject, back home he could never get to sleep until he'd seen the light of dawn, I'd wheel myself over to the window of the study and dream, I watched the darkness falter, heard the first rustling of pigeons, thought of J., Lépervier, myself, it seemed to me that we had managed to patch together a kind of raft to carry our happiness on, and now the more

I struggle to remember everything for J., the more I'm afraid, here I am transcribing death's agony, and in the end a comma can't ward off death for ever, and yet I have to get it all down, leave nothing out, for J., for Lépervier, for me, when he moved in six weeks ago, though the trip wasn't for another three weeks, it was the first time he'd come so early, and for the flash of an instant, just a flash, I saw J. transfixed in terror, and later, although Lépervier looked fine, she whispered that I was to think up every possible excuse to cancel my daily walks with him, I lied well, I felt weak, the weather was bad, a nightmare had upset me, but now lying is useless since Lépervier no longer wants to go out, in fact no longer can go out, he lies there half asleep, moaning quietly, he can't smoke any more so, just to give him a whiff, I light a cigarette and lay it in the ashtray by his bed, where it burns down on its own, he smiles at the aroma of the Gitane, I'm terrified, what if he dies before J. gets back, and that's not the worst of it, the worst is this constant struggle to beat back the jaws of death and not having the strength to keep at it, this not being able to relieve a friend's pain, three nights ago I almost called an ambulance but he refused, he murmured don't bother, if only J. would return, and then, in a broken voice, he told me of his one regret, a man he once loved, gone now, a man with four scars on his arm, four attempts at suicide, and Lépervier's one regret is that he learned the story behind only one of those scars, he told me not to forget to tell J. of his only regret, only one regret in a lifetime, he kept repeating, only one regret, I promised and that quieted him down and for an hour we were free of the threat of silence, yesterday I washed Lépervier, with a facecloth, the soap that smells like grapefruit, and the salad bowl, which I filled with lukewarm water, I had to go back and forth several times between his bed and the sink to keep the water from getting cold, I began with his feet and I worked my way up, his thighs, his belly, his sex, his chest, his back, his armpits, his head, his ears, an icon's frail nudity, I dressed him again in clean pyjamas, last night his teeth were chattering even though the house was warm, I dragged my own body alongside his, laid our legs together, and gently, very gently, I crooned a lullaby, Paul Lépervier my aged child, Paul Lépervier my only child, have no fear, don't be afraid, I'm here by your side and I'll never leave you, and almost inaudibly he repeated, have no fear, don't be afraid, I'm here by your side and I'll never leave you, and when the night finally slipped away we slept in each other's arms, I'm all right now, now we're ready for her

MISUNDERSTANDING IN SVENDBORG

The worst exiles are internal. Each year, to avoid suffocating, I find I must escape, get away from my narrow daily routine, travel. I select my destination entirely by chance, always mapping out the most convoluted route imaginable; why travel in a straight line when destiny is already such a dreary highway? My plane landed in Toronto an hour late and I missed my connection to Amsterdam; I was forced to wait five hours for the next flight and a further three hours, once I reached Skovelunde in Denmark, for my lost luggage to find me. When I had finally retrieved my suitcase, I was so groggy from fatigue that I failed to dodge the trunk lid which the taxi driver inadvertently slammed down on my head. Regaining consciousness a few minutes later, I weakly turned down the offer of two policemen to escort me to a nearby hospital. I have no memory of the train ride to Halsskov, other than the murmur of a stranger's voice informing me that the name of that city might be translated as "Forest-of-the-gorge". Nor do I recall anything of the ferry crossing to Svendborg on the island of Fyn: I felt as though I were vainly struggling to extricate myself from a spider's web drenched in fog.

Down by the port, twilight had softened the grey stones of the ancient façades. I strolled quietly, inhaling the briny fragrance of a gentle breeze. I decided to enter a peaceful cross-street; there was something about the strange way the windows of all the houses were adorned with either shutters or curtains of the very same crimson colour. One of them advertised modestly: *VAERLSE TIL LEJE*. I opened the door. Stepping over the threshold, I felt a shiver run through me, as though the Fates had breathed on the back of my neck. And yet the spruce colours and polished wood of the interior were no different from those of any other establishment in the country; there seemed to be no particular reason for concern.

In the minuscule salon adjoining the tidy reception area, a blind man with long blond hair was singing the blues and strumming, with both hands, a steel-stringed guitar which lay flat in his lap. Right next to him, a Japanese woman with half-shut eyes and carefully polished nails sat smoking from an ebony cigarette holder. Her knees of ivory and her dress of bright brocade had a slightly dizzying effect on me. Why did it suddenly occur to me that this delicate woman would despise the rain?

The proprietor materialized behind the counter with the discretion of a morning mist. The few oily hairs on his head, the greenish hue of his shark's teeth, the eczema spilling out of the collar of his scruffy shirt, and his repulsive obesity all combined to cause me some small degree of trepidation. As I do not speak the language, negotiations were laboriously complex; finally, it was in German that I was made to understand the very reasonable price of the room, but the man continued to try to explain I have no idea what to me, repeating over and over: *Vaerelse, eller krop til leje?** I put an end to the discussion by simply turning away and starting up the spiral staircase.

The next floor was bathed in semi-obscurity, but I had no difficulty finding both my room—thanks to the yawning door—and the capacious bed. I barely paused to unlace my shoes before collapsing into the blood-red glow of a single bedside light.

At first I thought I might still be dreaming. With astonishing regularity I heard couples going up and down the stairs, the squish of men's crêpe soles accompanying the clicking of stiletto heels, followed by keys turning in locks, whispers and joyless laughter.

I could not move an eyelash. I was engulfed in odours from the neighbouring rooms, swirling torrents of jasmine and lily of the valley, strange explosions of spikenard and ylang-ylang from which occasionally rose the sweet froth of orange blossom; then I began to detect a spray of cold ashes pulling against the undertow of bitter perspiration, and finally an acrid groundswell of fresh sperm coming off routed sheets. The mounting pain in my skull became a death threat. Whether it was the lethal fever or hallucinations I don't know, but I saw a hulking Neanderthal shaking the Japanese woman as though she were a rag doll, a mulatto woman curving her lips around the ardent stalk of a young pimpled dandy, a close-cropped redhead spreading open her shaved sex with her fingers under the gaze of a broken old man. Powerless, I lay that way, witness to all this miserable lovemaking, until a cerebral hemorrhage swept me into the realm of wailing shadows.

Faced with the prospect of endless wandering, I have chosen instead to become the phantom of the bordello. So that, when the first chink appears in the night, I may lay a sweet kiss on the finely spun eyelids of the girls.

---

*In Danish, "To rent a body or a room?"

23

# BODY OF SEASONS

Autumn

Do you remember, beautiful lover, when you came back to me this year? It was on a tree-covered walk on a cool August night. I had come, somewhat wearily, to a party given by an impresario in his immense garden on the slopes of the mountain; the saffron-coloured roses, heavy, as we all were, with the summer vapours, had already lowered their heads, and through their waning aroma, the tart scent of freshly cut grass rose like a piercing call. A warm but authentic Champagne was being served in flute glasses of scintillating crystal, and the touch of moonlight on luminous bodices was vaguely dizzying.

I did not hear my beautiful lover arrive, but I immediately recognized your kisses, the line of kisses you laid along the cleft of my black dress down to my hips. Naturally, it sent shivers through me and I shut my eyes to revel in your presence. I leaned against you, pleased to rediscover your scent of ripe apples and burnt wood, and stirred by the promise of an imminent feast pressing through the fabric against my rump.

We slipped away, using the rising wind as our excuse, and only the house cat, standing sentry in a window, marked our escape with the wink of a golden eye.

I laid my hand on your hip, you wrapped an arm

around my shivering shoulder, and as we walked along the edge of the park towards the city you talked of your last trip to Tierra del Fuego, six months ago, during that season when the animals put on fresh coats and spirits settle in for the winter. I was rocking gently to the sound of your voice and humming to myself, as I daydreamed about the cougar already flaming in your hidden mane.

We were surprised by a cold rain so dense that the deserted streets disappeared behind a shimmering silk canopy. Magician-like, you produced a claret-red umbrella, I pressed closer and we adjusted our pace to the water song. Your free hand played in my hair while I slipped my palm under your belt, in search of burning coals. No longer able to restrain my desire, I halted our walk, turned towards you, and pressed our bodies together, biting your mouth to force it open with delight. A sudden gust of wind tore away our umbrella and swept it, like some newly invented migratory bird, high into the sky and southward. We remained as we were, wrapped in a fierce embrace and drenched in heavenly rheum.

Then, lifting me in your arms as though I were as light as a leaf, you ran deep into the park beneath the shelter of an out-of-the-way tree, a maple I think, swaying, like us, in the storm.

I leaned my back against the rough bark, lifted my black dress to bare my thighs, and tore my panties in my hurry to offer you my frothing sex. You smiled and plunged like a phalanx inside me. Such roughness would normally turn me completely cold, but with you, my darling, it only fed my ardour, and I eagerly mounted pleasure's savage mare; but it was for you I longed, for you at your hardest, at your most tender. I broke away from my pleasure, from your caress, to free your taut scythe, to finger its desire. I wrapped a leg around your waist and to further fuel my fever, this time, ever so slowly, you entered me. At last everything was released: the night, our trembling flesh, the thunder, our sacred pleasure and our cries, our timeless cries.

Afterwards, still entwined and breathless, we raised our heads.

Above us, the tree had turned a scorched russet.

Winter

The snow is coming down.

How can I break your silence, pierce your defences?

I'll slip into my softest sweater, my red woollen stockings and my black silk garters, put on my boots of finest leather and, the satin lining of my old fur coat brushing against my bare belly, set out for your house. On the way, the wind grabs hold of my frozen cleft, and the cold wrenches tears from my eyes—at least I tell myself it's only the cold. At that moment I am reduced to the blur of a shadow, stripped as bare as the trees against the sky.

Devastating times: frozen blue winos huddling in the putrid breath of ventilation shafts, houses barricading themselves in with their secrets, the soul of the entire country muffled to its very fingertips.

It is snowing silence.

I'll enter your house through a crack in the door, pausing on the threshold just to breathe in the ordinary exhalations of your happiness: the comforting aroma of the stew you ate earlier, the magic bouquet of just-extinguished candles, the sharp trace of your last American cigarette. In the fireplace, the embers will murmur quietly; unafraid, the house cat shimmies up to my ankles girdled in frost. In the half-darkness I guess the shape of your body curled beneath a quilt. And then something inside flinches. Something breaks apart. Suddenly I am ashamed, ashamed of myself, of this underhanded way I have of possessing you. Like some wild nor'wester. Poor nor'wester, longing for the abyss.

You'll be asleep, I bend close to your face, my eyes slowly savouring—that strand of your hair adrift on the smooth surface of your cheek, your eyelids, translucent floes on a pair of violet lakes, your half-open mouth, which I absolutely will not allow myself to kiss.

On the white page of your bed, beneath the line of the sheet, I slide the length of your back, you shiver without waking while I bask in the warmth of your indolence. With my nails I tease your nipples, with my palm I cajole a hip, but then you stir and I have to wait for your dreams to dull your senses once again. Perhaps an hour runs down, drop by drop; for one hour I'll be a moraine to your glacier. Gently I lay a rosary of kisses from your head down to your loins; and then I slip along that tender coomb of flesh between your thighs, I brush against your testicles, until my fingers, polarized, magnetized, close around your phallus, and slowly, very slowly I pull you into ecstasy.

The perfume of your milk will be like a fresh wound.

You have slept through it all, or so I tell myself, since you haven't granted me so much as a glance.

The snow is coming down, curtains of crystalline despair.

The light is dying, night engulfs us, why this bleeding crater where my heart should be, why are you the only one who can cure it?

Beautiful lover, why so cold?

Spring

When everyone's feet are soaking in the slush of misery, and the poor are shivering in badly heated rooms, I am like this country, I can no longer bear the winter, nor its breath heavy with solitude.
But it's you, my beautiful lover, I long for most.
It will be in the morning. On this morning, for the first time, the buds on the birch tree in the yard will burst open like a thousand eyelids. I hear a crow, quicker than her sisters, proclaiming a freshness in the air, an irresistible lightness, a new light full of the scent of hope. This morning, under my tongue I have a taste for maple sugar, between my thighs a desire for sap rising, and, especially, in my heart a terrible thirst for the spring floods of love.
This morning, I ignore the newspapers and their columns blackened with blood; instead I enjoy a poem by Michel Beaulieu, then slip into my sylphine shoes and that flowered dress which has been pining away deep in the closet for so many months. Then I tear the plastic sheets, miserable glaucoma, from all the windows, and hang my freshly washed sheets on the line, so many banners emblazoned with your name and flying in the open air.
This morning, even despair breaks into song.
In my street the Portuguese women hum quietly as they sweep the scraps abandoned by the cold from their doors, the alleycats come begging more than ever for their share of caresses, the laughing winos are rocking on the playground swings: every look, every stone radiates deliverance.
And you come to me—hair tousled, hands overflowing with umbellate flowers—you wrap your arms around me and whisper: "Look at our garden: the lambs

exulting in the dew, springs leaping with jubilation, apple tree blossoms like the pink lace dresses of young girls."

You'll take me in your silken arms and bare my shoulders, rain down a shower of kisses, and continue:

"Most of all, look at our children, this gold cast from our two bodies, these victories torn from a millennium of evil, these souls snatched from us, but also from death: look at Gabrielle, our first-born, full of the blondness of my laugh and the dark shadows in your eyes. And next to her look at Habéké from Burundi, frail survivor of the Tutsi guns, and Emmanuella from Chile, whose mother was cut to pieces in a prison cell. Look at the hungry, the abandoned, whom together we will love."

And then once more, to celebrate our wellspring, I wrap myself around your hips, and once more your phalanx, your shaft, drives my dark corolla into frenzy, and once more, once more, you and I put on our wings of joy.

I love you so much, springtide of dreams!

Summer

Listen: the next door neighbour's languid and invisible saxophone, the children announcing their happy holidays, the cicadas chirring greetings, the city's ten thousand choruses shouting themselves hoarse to welcome your return.

Look: the supine cat upon the floor, her pupils luminous with fever, the exhausted blades of the fan slowly spinning, the lace curtains barely fluttering: the whole house seems to be liquefying, dreaming of the ocean.

I can no longer bear the searing heat in the air, and in

my soul; this morning, again, the lash of desire lacerated my heart.

Tonight, when you come to me like the tide in the powdered tangerine sunset, in the air thick with the cries of wildfowl and the flavours of salt, tonight at last I'll unfurl like a sail thirsty for wind.

And then this is what my beautiful love says:

"Against January's glacial tyranny, I stroke the small hairs on the nape of your neck; against November's long drizzle, I lay my lips on your wrist; against March's bitter sleet, I tease your left earlobe; against the sixty thousand different poisons infecting the river, I kiss your petalled eyelids; against the cunning emanations of biphenyl polychloride, dioxins and furans, I am a swarm of hummingbirds pecking at your neck; against hidden violence, against bad fathers who abuse their daughters, I offer a mouthful of water from my mouth to yours; against the infinite solitude of winos, my eyelashes caress your ankles; against Native American misery wrapped in hideous contempt, my fingers tickle your ivory knees; against overt and covert racism, I fondle the hollow of your navel; against the torturers of South America, my tongue traces the border of your hip; against intolerance and religious fanaticism, I hem the curve of your breasts with kisses; against the blind hum of nuclear and chemical missiles, I palm the gorge between your thighs into a froth."

Then you said no more, nor did I, and under the moon's Cheshire-cat smile we harnessed the rapture of our bodies intertwined. For children's sun-drenched laughter. For the maple sugar of maternal kindness. For the perfumed opulence of friendships between women. For all the ecologists, pacifists, discoverers of vaccines, soldiers of happiness and warriors of joy. For the fruition of hope, we have harnessed rapture.

And again in the first light of day, we told ourselves: "Against death and all its glutinous nets, our only weapon, our strength, is love."

THE INSEMINATION OF THE SKY

Sunday, March 15

How I love the dawn. Every dawn. This is also my miniature poodle Paradox's favourite time for her walk. The rosy glow of the street lamps still erodes the darkness. Napoleon Street hardly breathes beneath an uncertain sky. Silence, at last, appeases the community. One could almost forget that, elsewhere, war. . . .

Today there was a surprising softness in the air, like ancient muslin, I even removed my hood the better to feel its caress. What's more, on the sidewalk, still cluttered with ice, I noticed several mismatched mittens, along with three abandoned woollen caps. These are the signs of spring's swift approach.

Paradox was jogging gaily along in the windless calm. That dog is never happier than when she is alone with me. Any other presence, even an acquaintance or a mere pigeon, petrifies her. I was therefore rather surprised to hear her howling with all her might at a large sheet of paper fluttering above Boulevard Saint-Laurent. How could this shred of newspaper draw such lovely arabesques in the motionless air? As I watched, fascinated by the capricious dance, the sheet suddenly threw itself directly at me. As though it had a mind of its own. I could not avoid it; it flattened itself against my face and, for a few seconds, I was suffocating in some grainy, slightly gummy material that smelled of forest undergrowth. And then . . . in a flash, the thing simply disintegrated. I might have convinced myself that I'd dreamed the whole incident had it not been for Paradox, who was standing transfixed and staring at me with a perplexed look.

April 3

I'm so thirsty, I am constantly drinking water and I take several showers a day. I feel strangely detached from all those things that used to upset me—the unjustifiable killing, the violence, whether public or personal, the lack of love. . . . What is happening to me?

Today I experienced a truly unexpected pleasure: while I was listening to Richard Desjardins's song, "Nataq", suddenly the taste of dark creamy chocolate cake soaked in orange liqueur filled my mouth. The taste remained on my tongue exactly the length of the song.

April 11

I'm neglecting my friends. Am I losing even my heart?

At the same time, the bouts of confusion between my senses continue, and with increasing frequency. Constantly, in fact. Eating yogurt, I have the sensation of being rubbed from head to toe with a soft woollen fabric. Or the stink of a truck's exhaust produces the unpleasant screech of a fork on a blackboard in my ears. Or then again, when I stroke Paradox, for as long as I'm touching her coat, I see nothing but the oranges of Chagall's painting *Paris Seen from a Window*! Very troubling.

My doctor has diagnosed a "spectacular synesthesia" and recommends I consult a psychiatrist. The idiot. He can't even see the inevitable.

April 15

I can no longer work, it's become impossible to concentrate. The only place I make any effort is here in my journal, I don't really know why it seems so important to document the progress of this, my. . . . What? My illness? My metamorphosis? My disappearance?
It's raining buckets. I came home soaked. As long as I was wet I could hear the echo of a Gregorian chant.
During the night one of my little toes, the left one, changed colour and texture. I can still feel it, although the blood seems to have entirely gone out of it and the skin looks like very fine whitish sponge. I am thirstier and thirstier.

April 21

Paradox refuses to play with me.
All my toes are blanched, and speckled brown. I desire nothing more than to contemplate the sky for hours on end, submerged in lavender and ocean scents, the unhurried harmonies of cellos, milk and honey, raw silk between my legs. . . .
Even dying, the idea of dying, no longer torments me.

May 11

It continues to rain. I have shrunk by twenty centimetres or so, I look like a caricature of a giant mushroom. My head and right hand are not yet affected. My legs are almost welded together: I can still walk but with some difficulty. I have found a quiet corner on the Mountain, a bird sanctuary on the Westmount side, where I shall plant myself in a grove of young birches, next to a dying aspen. We'll have peace there. Paradox should survive for perhaps a year: I'll try to bring along a couple of ten-kilo bags of dog food, the beef flavour, which smells like the scales of a badly tuned piano. I shall leave nothing behind: tonight I'll set fire to the house. Tomorrow, this will become an imaginary journal.

The middle of the winter, more or less

The dog is well sheltered at my foot.
Neither snow nor cold troubles us.

My memory dissipating.
No regrets.

Feast of clouds, symphony of stars, oh infinite joy.
I long for spring when I too can release my spores.

A THOUSAND AND ONE MINOTAURS

*F*or some time now, a long time, I have wanted to go to that city. It's a big city full of life, several thousand people live there, any stranger can come in.*

In the midst of her feeling of helplessness, the words of the book read like omens. For twenty-seven years she had taken counsel from these biblical pages. That morning she had removed the volume from its cardboard case, soiled and patched with yellowed tape. She had opened it at random, as was her custom. And that was what the book had told her. She shuddered, *La Gazette* had just informed her of the death of Mylène. So she would have to abandon everything, go into the big city and catch the murderer. She had no choice in the matter.

Mylène had been strangled. Under a full moon. Her darling Mylène.

Memories, shattering intimacies. She had met her in the infirmary, sweeping under her bed. Following a failed attempt at suicide, Mylène lay sobbing into her pillow. The sick were subject to less surveillance, and in those few days a strange bond, coloured by a mutual bitterness and compassion, had formed between the child and the

---

*All quotations in italic are taken from *Récits et Fragments*, by Franz Kafka. Translated from the French by R.M.

forty-year-old woman, between the rebel and the widow. And then Mylène had escaped from Saint Brigid, or "Plain and Rigid" as the teenagers called it, and with good reason: a maximum security reform school is not a place where hearts soar. During the past three months she had often thought of Mylène out there, free. And now the abyss.

She had handed her letter of resignation to the director. No regrets. She had always despised his severity. Their unspoken trench war was finally at an end. Even then, with his usual sneering contempt, he had taken a kind of sour pleasure in pointing out that a cleaning lady is easily replaced. She had said goodbye to the other employees: the eldest had cried, the youngest had given her an aventurine-coloured scarf for luck. A mighty thin talisman to track a faceless monster.

Beyond the squat palisades of the Centre, the wind was lashing at the tender fields. This year, spring had been slow in coming. She set out for the station in the village without a backward glance. Behind her she was leaving her miserable, sunless living quarters and a shabbily framed photograph of her wedding. Behind her. She had brought nothing but the precious book and her meagre savings, which she had hidden among its pages. Behind her, twenty-seven years of scrubbing floors and scraping sinks, twenty-seven years of grey widowhood, slag grey, empty grey. Why is it that for some people the wheels of happiness seem hopelessly derailed? She had been a young newlywed when a heart attack had taken her husband. In the book she pried from his stiffening fingers, she had read: *He was a citizen of neither the penitentiary nor of the State to which it belonged.* She was only nineteen. At the time, the reform school was still preparing to receive its first delinquents, and was looking for maintenance staff. So she had chained her destiny to the bars of Plain and Rigid. The worst prisons are locked beneath one's skin.

The crowd at the bus terminus in the city stank of solitude. In the Centre the girls had used the toilet cubicles as letter drops. Here in the women's washroom, only the cubicle equipped for wheelchairs was free. A runaway without money would have taken refuge in here. The cold metal walls were bare of graffiti. Under the cover of the waste basket someone had scrawled an arrow pointing skyward. On the ceiling the soundproof tiles were cracked from the humidity. Standing on the toilet tank, on a hunch, she had slipped her hand through the broken corner of a tile. A neatly folded paper seemed to be waiting there for her, with a typed message:

Bist Du allein? Ohne Freund? Ohne Geld? Ich bin für Dich da. Tu es perdue? Sans ami? Sans argent? Je suis là pour toi. Are you alone? Not a friend in the world? No money? I can help you.

Joe

There was a phone number. When she called, Joe answered immediately. These days even buzzards carry cellular phones, so as not to miss out on a single victim. She disguised her voice and lied about her age, confessing to a helpless fifteen. Joe told her to meet him in a quarter of an hour, in the station snack bar. There was something ugly about the way the man whispered, like a November drizzle.

In the greasy spoon, a harried waitress served pale faces under a dirty neon light. The coffee was undrinkable. Next to her, a foul-smelling bum muttered obscenities. A lone fly battered itself against the window. It was as though time were coagulating and the world had drifted into nightmare. A man appeared. That air of nonchalance, the brutal mug, the predatory look: Joe. He scanned the room for his prey. No teenagers. He took off. She followed, but he disappeared into a black limousine driven by a shadow. She caught a glimpse of a decal in the rear window: the foaming, raging head of a bull.

Disconcerted, she began walking north, in the direction the car had sped. She should have taken the licence-plate number. She seemed unable to concentrate. A warmed-over, fetid breeze spilled down her neck. An ambulance wailed down a cross-street. A little farther on, she was inexplicably drawn to a bar whose lights were still burning, the Styx.

A fog of milky cigarette smoke, a clicking dance of billiard balls on two pool tables, forty or so rickety tables around which an assortment of suspicious young malcontents were busy drinking themselves into a stupor: the Styx was packed, in spite of the late hour. She found a seat a long way from the bar, ordered a glass of mineral water from an obese and stinking waiter, and sank into a gloomy reverie.

He slid into the seat beside her with the discretion of a cat and whispered: *A frail widow all dressed in black with a straight skirt stood perfectly still in the room . . .* Ariel! She'd have recognized that broken voice anywhere. Her soul leapt, out of surprise as much as joy. Had she once been in love with him? He in his twenties. She over forty. Two years ago, to pay his way through school, he had worked one short summer at Plain and Rigid as a security guard. Ariel's shift had begun as her own hard day's labour came to an end. Every evening she would go by his locker; they'd discuss Kafka and then, without fail, when they were through talking, he would untie his long red hair for her. She'd plunge her rough hands into the stream of glittering light and for several hours afterwards her palms would be full of the tenuous aroma of happiness. She past forty. He in his twenties. Had she been in love? In spite of the muggy weather, his hair hung loose; she could have reached over and wiped the line of sweat off his brow with the tips of her fingers, but she didn't dare. Weariness had darkened his translucent complexion. He was studying for a Master's degree; his love of literature, combined with unemployment, had driven him to work as an informer for the police morality and drug squad. The fact that he was so glaringly visible allowed him to move freely in the underworld without arousing suspicion. "Tropical fish camouflage," he told her with a pained smile. Unbeknownst to his superiors, he had decided to unmask a mysterious crack trafficker who ran a ring using children as pushers and prostitutes. Six investigators had been shot down when they had come too close to the source of the ring. The trail faded here, at the Styx, where, according to Ariel, you could buy anything: knives, guns, hard or soft drugs, the soft flesh of girls or boys. She could see it was useless to try to dissuade him from his mission. They fell silent. Through the stench in the Styx she could make out the aroma of rosemary from his wild mane of hair. But the fire-brand of her vengeance turned away all tender feelings. *La Gazette* having provided no details of Mylène's death, she questioned Ariel. He blanched. She insisted. He refused to say a word. She demanded the truth. Finally, Ariel paid for their drinks and, laying a hand on her shoulder, led her outside. The sky was heavy with the threat of a storm.

They walked towards the south-west until they came to a sinister-looking building with dark windows: they were standing before the daunting headquarters of the Provincial Police. In the entrance to the underground garage, a pale-faced attendant in a glass booth waved half-heartedly at Ariel. They passed through the deserted morgue. The refrigerators whirred, imperturbable; somewhere a broken neon light crackled. Powerful antiseptic fumes coming off the red stone floor made her dizzy. Ariel unlocked his tiny office and closed the door behind them. From a damaged locker he produced the photo of Mylène's remains, along with those of four other girls of approximately the same age, who had been killed in the same way: sliced open from the vulva to the neck, and strangled with a section of intestine. In all four cases, Ariel told her, pathological examinations had revealed signs of advanced malnutrition, severe crack intoxication and numerous lesions in the vaginal and rectal areas. She could not help asking why he kept these horrible pictures. "To keep my commitment from flagging," he murmured. She decided to remain silent about her own plan. She listened to each syllable of that cracked voice as though it were the last time she would hear it.

They separated an hour before dawn. It had rained; a light fog was rising off the street as she watched him disappear down a greasy alley. How much longer would that flaming head of hair burn?

She was tempted to go after him, to feel once more the weight of his arm around her shoulder; didn't she deserve just a hint of tenderness? The book was categorical: *So I stood, leaning against the moonlit wall of a house, and waited.*

A few metres away, a dirty syringe lay amid the garbage. The Fates had provided the fatal weapon. She wrapped the needle in a bit of filthy paper and stuffed it into her pocket. Now, into the labyrinth.

She slept in the street for the next three weeks, not wanting to exhaust her financial resources. Why? She had no idea, except that something told her the money would be put to better use later. She slept during the day, on park benches; when it rained, she took refuge in the subway. She managed to clean herself up, more or less, in the fountains. There had been a couple of festivals downtown: the wastebaskets were overflowing with bits of sandwiches and scraps of pizza. The sidewalks and brick façades shimmered behind the veil of her thirst. At night she searched for the limousine with the bull. She was methodical. If necessary she would follow every boulevard, every street, out to the edges of the most distant suburbs. Tenacity was all she had left for a name.

At the full moon, another child had been slain. No one seemed particularly shocked.

The rain had been coming down for the last nine days, a heavy rain, bringing no relief from the heat and cleansing nothing. The sky lay over the buildings like a coat of lead. She was filthy, exhausted. Hungry. Ariel had not come back to the Styx. Which meant that, along with everything else, she was worrying. Mired in worrying.

She had begun to doubt, to doubt the success of her mission. Her only clue, fleeting and uncertain, was the limousine, that night-owl. She read: *There was a soldier there whose task it was to observe the enemy.* That convinced her that Joe was merely the assassin's hireling. But how could she hope to face the murderer when she lacked even the strength to wrestle her own sorrow? How could she succeed where the police had foundered? The acrid taste of failure filled her mouth.

Once again, the book took charge: *[. . .] he must [. . .] not only swallow his despair but persevere with his hard labour.*

She could not give up.

Summer had melted over the city, feverish, mind-numbing. Before moving out to the outskirts of town, she decided to investigate the underground garages beneath the highrises. It was surprisingly easy to get in. Every watchman will occasionally drift. She stood before those regiments of steel lined up in the foul air as though she were contemplating the dismal landscape of her life. Why had death crushed her innocence so long ago, and then refused to relent, taking Mylène from her, Mylène whose infrequent smiles had cracked a light in her heart?

She entered the underground parking of La Cité's three towers through the shopping centre on the ground floor. Beneath luxury lay desolation, as usual. Level A of the garage contained a few hundred vehicles, a network of sweating pipes along the low ceiling and a gigantic fan that filled the air with a constant and deafening roar. Whenever a car passed, she hid behind a column or crouched down against a bumper. And then she was staring dumbfounded at the bull's head limousine and she knew the gods had decided to favour her mission. There was no free spot, so the driver had to go down to level B. She raced down the rusty iron fire escape. A quick glance told her this floor was also full. She plunged again, floor after floor, down to level F. Breathless, she almost missed Joe as he vanished into the service elevator, dragging a terrified teenager by the arm.

She climbed the six staircases as quickly as she could, but in the hall a cantankerous doorman with a face full of warts intercepted her and refused her access to the apartment elevators. Discouraged, she returned to the caverns below.

Each Cerberus she encountered on her way seemed fiercer than the last; she could not get past them. She slept on level E, in a narrow passageway between two doors, an architectural blunder. An Arab dishwasher from the barbecue restaurant put the customers' scrapings aside for her. But anxiety was eating away at her. One evening, in the hallway, she noticed an Asian woman with chapped hands smelling of caustic soda. Most likely a cleaning attendant. She followed the foreigner to a bus stop, where she managed to explain, not without considerable difficulty—language proved to be yet another barrier—that she was looking for a kidnapped child. She begged the woman to let her take over her job for one week: this was her last chance. Her tears turned out to be less convincing than her savings. Removing the eight hundred-dollar bills from her book, she discovered the phrase: *A woman's experience would be required here,* which made her decision irrevocable. The two cleaning ladies returned to La Cité. The employee showed her where her things were kept, and left her a set of keys before vanishing into the night. The moon was growing rounder, menacing.

Six days passed, six days without a glimpse of sky, as she lugged her heavy cart through the corridors, spying on everything as she scrubbed. Tomorrow, the full moon. Tomorrow, urgency.

The thirteenth, she was almost certain, was the right floor. The beige carpet had been replaced with tiles covered in an unintelligible design. Why, if not for some unspeakable reason, had every sign been erased—the apartment numbers, even the emergency exits, were gone—why had the architecture been altered so that it was impossible not to lose one's way? No music, not a sound filtered out of the apartments; this silence stank. How to lay an ambush for the killer? And where?

She had no illusions that her mop might suddenly uncover a tide of blood pouring from beneath a door, but she knew that sometimes mere dust can tell tales. She had washed the tiles, on her knees. Methodically. From time to time heavy-lidded men passed her in the hall, paying no more attention to her than they would have to a dog. She consoled herself in the familiar scent of ammonia: her vengeance would be a purification.

After five hours of hard toil, she finally uncovered a clue. Pinned behind the lower hinge of a door, a thin lock of red hair dangled. Trembling, she pulled it free. Held it up to her face. How she had wanted to be wrong. Alas, it was Ariel's rosemary scent, Ariel's sunset red. For the hair to have been caught in the lower hinge like that, his beautiful head had to have been dragged across the floor. She hoped his agony had not lasted long, that pain had not been his final companion.

She laid a strand of her mop on the doorframe so as not to make a mistake when she returned, and went to put her cart away in the closet by the elevators. She used the Asian woman's skeleton key to get inside the studio. Inside: furniture of modern design, full of aggressive, pointed angles; a collection of antique surgical instruments in an aluminum frame, an unmade bed covered in bespattered sheets, thick wine-coloured curtains, overflowing ashtrays. A set of chains with handcuffs had been screwed into the back wall of the bathroom, a metre and a half from the ceiling. In the kitchen, the cupboards were all bare. She crawled under the sink, tucking her knees under her chin.

She fell asleep to the intermittent gurgling of the pipes. She is lying in the belly of an ancient pyramid, a shrivelled mummy in her sarcophagus, surrounded by her golden gem-encrusted jewellery, funerary urns containing her embalmed organs, and bas-reliefs relating her exploits. All around her the jungle is in flames, filled with the sounds of screaming monkeys, panic-stricken, screeching macaws and growling panthers trapped by the fire. A distant laughter begins by scratching at her ear, then swells, and finally wakes her completely. From the back of the apartment she can hear the rattle of chains, someone breathing heavily. Cursing herself for having fallen asleep, she quietly emerges from her hiding-place and straightens painfully. Stars dance before her eyes. She can barely stand. This is no time to falter. The air is heavy with the scent of warm blood. Anguish burns in her throat. The chains knock against each other, the panting grows more rapid. She tiptoes out of the kitchen. The room is sinking into shadows. Feeling her way, she unplugs and grabs hold of a massive bedside lamp. A stark gash of light outlines the doorsill of the bathroom. Not daring to breathe, she opens the door a crack. A pool of blood is creeping across the tiles. A child hangs by her wrists, her hair plastered pathetically against her face. She has been gagged with a rag. Her eyes are wide open, staring down. Too late. Too late. The child has already been torn open. The horrible wound is hidden by the hairy body of a naked man, squirming and giggling over the corpse. He is on the verge of ejaculating. She smashes the lamp down on the back of his head. He staggers, bellows. The entrails of the child fall with an awful slapping sound. She has not hit the killer hard enough; she tries again with all the violence of her rage. He does not move. She undoes her aventurine-coloured scarf and wraps it round the tormentor's arm. In the crook of the elbow a vein bulges, beating still. She takes the syringe from her pocket. Fills it with air. She strikes the vein, sends the air racing to the heart, retracts the plunger, pushes more air in. Four or five times. The man shudders. His whole body tenses in a final spasm.

She feels no joy. She looks down at the prognathic features of the stranger, the narrow forehead overrun by thick eyebrows, the flat nose, the drooling lip. A cruel, bovine lout. She feels no joy. Only a weariness in her soul. Why go on living. She opens her book. *The accomplishment is never complete*, it tells her.

That's it, then. One less minotaur. How many thousands more?

THE POSSESSION OF JACQUES BRAISE

Ah, the blondness of some men! My name is Jacinthe-Pierre O'Bamsawé, I was born forty-five long hard winters ago, of a Haitian mother and an Abenaki father, and blondness always leaves me speechless. When it doesn't completely annihilate me. This is the story of the error a blond man tattooed across my mouth, hard luck for his soul.

It was one of those autumn evenings that are too warm to be trusted. Three months earlier, I had sold one of my erotic sketches, for a paltry sum, to a cultural magazine, which had subsequently invited me to a party celebrating its founding anniversary. At first I had planned not to go: my true exile begins the moment I am separated from my painting—I would much rather lose myself in a *trompe-l'oeil* than in the bottom of a glass—but, well, on that particular evening I felt a need to contemplate the misery of others rather than my own. Sooner or later, every hermit falters. The party was being held at the Falsification, a bar on Saint-Hubert, you know, the one where, rather than sitting on wooden chairs, you find yourself sinking mercilessly into long, winding sofas of snow-white leather? The moon had punched a hole in the sky, Montreal was reeling in a gusting wind. I arrived at three minutes to midnight, the hour of the long knives and she-wolves.

The room was overflowing with the under-thirty

crowd, all dressed up to look ragged and marginal; on the other hand, the lighting was turned down low, which was a great help to my makeup (a bit of white folks' magic, in exchange for a few brown bills, but then again, without a dose of illusion, where would I be?) And of course there he was, like July in the middle of grey November, engrossed in a heated discussion with what looked like a Venetian prince. A journalist acquaintance whispered to me: "The blond one is Jacques Braise." My heart leapt: I knew the name since I had been devouring his bittersweet weekly columns for some time. I managed to flop down next to him. I forgot all about alcohol; I just sat there drinking in his blondness.

    Quite by accident, I swear, I plucked three hairs from the back of his black cashmere jacket; I wrapped them in the aluminum foil from my cigarette pack and placed them carefully in the side pocket of my handbag. Once my treasure was hidden away, I was overcome by a strange lethargy, and I shut my eyes. It was as though I had done nothing, as though some evil spirit which I could not resist had acted in my stead. I did not speak, I was savouring every second, and an hour passed before Jacques Braise finally turned to me. He seemed pleased to learn who I was; he ordered champagne and talked passionately about his writing until dawn. I drank more of the music of his voice than alcohol. And those eyes the colour of dark blue bruises: I was bewitched. Gallantly, he offered to walk me home through the near-empty streets, as though there were a beast living or dead that could frighten me. A terrible storm raged within me, the culmination of all my woes, as though only he, Jacques Braise, could deliver me from them. And then, on my doorstep, hard luck for his soul, his lips brushed mine for one moment's breath.

    There are women, perhaps the more solitary kind,

whom a single fleeting kiss can set ablaze: I am one of those women.

And so I did my best to see him again. I telephoned the magazine several times. The receptionist blocked my calls. I wrote to him several times. He never answered my letters. Anyone else would have given up, perhaps shed a few tears over dashed desire, and returned to her life without hope, but not I. I am tenacious, dangerous, and completely crazy. Jacques Braise refused to give himself willingly to me. Too bad. I would steal him.

I found the recipe in my mother's old book of spells, between Ardent Waters and the Elixir of Jealousy. I began with the first ingredient, and for once I was sorry capital punishment had been abolished. Failing that, I kept an eye on the news-in-brief column in the *Journal de Montréal* until, one Saturday morning, I found what I was looking for: a farmer by the name of Ubald Lusignan, from the tiny village of Saintes-Plaies, just north of the city, had committed suicide. According to the article, the man, a childless widower whose farm had been seized by his creditors, had hanged himself from a branch of an oak tree outside his front door. With a sigh, I took the bus to Saintes-Plaies. So much work, so much time spent away from my oils! But my lips were on fire; I had to soothe the pain.

A soft, dirty snow was falling. In the convenience store on the town's only street, an employee, a hatchet-faced boy with a sly, unpleasant look, gave me the once-over before telling me the way to Croche Road, way out in the countryside. I walked a long time before I found Ubald Lusignan's house; on the way I broke the heel of one of my fine leather boots. The farm, with its weeds and dilapidated shutters, reeked of desolation. Even the ancient oak tree was praying to the heavens. I had a terrible time digging in the hard ground beneath the tree, but I found what I was searching for and unearthed it. The mandrake, which is always so disquieting with its look of a bleached doll, seemed almost to be snickering. I broke off its left arm, carefully wrapped it in a bit of silver foil from my cigarette pack, and put it away with the three hairs. The remainder of the root I buried again in the same hole. You never know, someone else might be needing it; one should always think of others. . . .

I had less difficulty locating the second ingredient. Mama and Papa had always told me: "If you should ever need us, don't be shy, that's what we're here for." It was now or never. I made my way to the South Shore. Under the river, during the dreary subway ride, I thought about my prey and tried to talk some sense into myself: he's twenty years my junior, what use does a good-looking boy like that have for a gold-toothed half-breed, a forty-year-old with hair already going grey, leave him to the world of the living. But by now the back of my neck and shoulders were burning up, what choice did I have? I had to go on.

It was freezing in the cemetery, and the moon was waning in a silent wind. I found the old dwarf, looking as always so solemn in his dark suit, and he brought me the three-metre ladder. As he turned away, he whispered in his deep baritone, "I'll be back in an hour to close up." It was a Monday evening, so there would be no one around. Perfect.

I scrambled up onto the highest rung of the ladder, from where I could just reach the upper alcove of the columbarium. A square of constellations shone down through the skylight above my head. I opened the tiny glass door, chipping a nail in the process. I grabbed the copper case shaped like a bible, turned it over, pulled the

Phillips screwdriver from my bag, and undid the four cross-head screws. I removed the base. Good evening, Wounded Bear O'Bamsawé, my father of mountain springs and forests. Good evening, Pierre-Josephine Aristide, my mother of fire and fruit. I allowed myself a moment to caress two fragments of charred bone, one for her and one for him. I thought back to my childhood, those happy days rocking in a cradle of legends more ancient than any civilization, stories from a time when the gods could still touch us with their hands. But I did not linger long; I removed a sprinkling of ash, a pinch from her side, a pinch from his, wrapped it in a sheet of glistening foil from my cigarette pack, and tucked it away with the three strands of hair and segment of root in my bag. Then I replaced the bottom of the funerary urn and reshelved it in its niche. As a token of thanks I left an open flask of oil of gardenia, before hurrying away to catch my bus on the half-hour. I could have taken any dead person's ashes, since nothing is kept under lock and key inside the mausoleum. But that would not have been wise; I can think of no more certain way to drown oneself in a flood of nightmares.

    Montreal may be nothing but a jungle of iniquity, but this has its advantages. For the third ingredient of my charm I went to the Eleventh Eden, on the corner of Saint-Grégoire and Papineau, a discothèque barred to anyone over eighteen. It was Sunday: the city was bursting with cold and the sunlight slashed like a razor across faces and walls. The doorman, a gorilla with a vicious face, refused to let me in. I showed him my sketch pad and explained that I wanted to do some drawings of young people dancing. Art can sometimes serve as a good excuse, or even unlock a door.

    Inside, the kaleidoscopic spotlights were spinning and

the rock music was deafening; I took refuge in a corner as far as possible from the speakers. I took out my pad and a mechanical pencil with a soft, thick lead. Almost as soon as I began to draw, I was surrounded by a swarm of young women all eager to pose. I sketched furiously, distributing portraits as I completed them; each young woman, as she posed, talked about herself, her life, her everyday woes and cares. I listened to their babbling, all the while waiting and watching for my victim. At last she stood before me: twelve years old—"and a half", she insisted—with a lovely name, Mimosa, a name which could not have been less suited to her obesity and spotty complexion. She seemed uncomfortable; under my persistent questioning, and not without some considerable hesitation, she finally admitted, in a whisper, that she was menstruating and worried about staining her dress, and that, bad luck, she had no money to buy a fresh sanitary napkin from the machine. I dropped my pad and pencil and followed the teenager to the toilet. I dropped a coin in the dispenser, and Mimosa took her packet into the seventh cubicle. Meanwhile, I took the opportunity to touch up my eye makeup: by now the fire had spread to my chest; it had drawn tears and made my kohl run. I managed to scratch my cornea with my ivory eyeliner pencil. How I wish I knew what makes my desire so implacable.

    Mimosa scurried back to join the wriggling and twitching on the dance floor and I slipped into the seventh cubicle. I opened the white metal box and retrieved the napkin, which was soaked in lovely clear blood. With the golden scissors bequeathed to me by my mother and strictly reserved for witchcraft, I cut out a blood-soaked corner of the napkin, enveloped it in shining cigarette foil and stowed it away in the compartment of my bag. I was truly nauseated, but some demon, I don't know which, had forced me over my feelings of disgust. The worst was yet to come.

Soon I was incapable of sleep; the fire scorched my back right down into my loins. I needed a rat. Back in Petit-Goâve I need only have bent over, but in Montreal I had to bide my time until three o'clock in the morning in order to raise a manhole cover on the corner of Saint-Laurent and Rachel. I worked quickly; I did not want to be surprised by the police. Oh, I had tried to obey the law, to get permission to go down during regular hours, but without exception the municipal employees turned out to be highly uncooperative, even belligerent. For three days I had wandered from one office to the next, only to run up against closed doors and barely polite rejections. As the time of the full moon approached, I was forced, reluctantly, to abandon these futile attempts and resort to crime. I donned my worn leather jacket, thigh boots and heavy motorcycle gloves—for a moment I was twenty again and astride my Harley Davidson. I brushed nostalgia aside; this was no time for soft-heartedness.

Under the street the stink was terrible but the temperature was pleasantly warm. I turned off my flashlight. The glow of a street lamp filtered through the manhole cover. I gazed at the stream of filth, removed a morsel of still bloody filet mignon from my bag, squatted down on the narrow walkway with my left hand extended, and waited, absolutely motionless. I thanked my father for having taught me, when I was barely nine years old, to fish for trout bare-handed in the powerful current of the crystal-clear Kitchigama river. In those days life was a simple matter of survival, every second was filled with the urgency of the present, the future was silent, free of suffocating questions, and my dreams had not yet begun to poison my waking hours—in those days I knew how to live. These ruminations were cut short by a slippery head rising above the brackish water. His eyes gleamed like Sardinian agates. I could see him sniffing the piece of meat from a distance. He didn't move. He eyed me with suspicion. I had stopped breathing. I was as impassive as a mountain. We remained that way, studying each other, for a hundred years. At last he swam towards me. Ever so slowly. He slid up out of the water onto the slimy walkway. Slowly, cautiously, he edged towards me. He raised himself on his hind legs. Looking at the ratty grey fur on his belly, I could tell that this rodent was no spring chicken. Like lightning he leapt at the scrap of beef. Even more quickly, I grabbed him by the neck. He let loose a piercing shriek, twisted and turned to get free. Implacably I squeezed his throat with both hands. He tried to bite me, ripping at my gloves with his terrible incisors. I did not loosen my grip. With one swift twist of the wrist I cracked his skull against the pavement. After that, prying his jaws open and tearing his tongue out was child's play. I tossed the carcass into the fetid waters, wiped the bit of blood on the cement and soaked the inside of a bit of brilliant cigarette foil with the rat's saliva. Now, at last, I had everything I needed.

    I hurried home as quickly as I could to unwrap all my shimmering papers. With my golden scissors I sliced Jacques Braise's three hairs into tiny pieces. I mixed this light dust with the mandrake root, the ashes of the dead, the virgin's menstrual blood and the rat's spit. Then it was pound and stir, pound and stir, and add just a touch of not quite fresh egg yolk to bind it all. I was furious: how I longed to live free of obsessions, but I've never had the strength to dig in and resist cyclones, I end up jumping into the saddle and riding them out. . . .

Once the potion had been reduced for thirteen hours in a slow cooker, I placed the remaining precious drop in the hollow tiger's eye stone of an Italian ring, a gift that my friend Ada Lazuli picked up during one of her European tours. I had never dared to use the ring, which, it seems, once belonged to the Borgia woman; but in love and war. . . .

The next day, around five in the afternoon, I waited for Jacques Braise in the Pégase des Ténèbres, one of those hot bars full of flash and noise, this one next to the office of the cultural magazine. I was drinking mineral water; the fiery craving had descended into my digestive tract. My man never showed. I came again the next day and every day after that. Inexorably, a little more each evening, the winter solstice engulfed us all. A week passed before Jacques Braise walked into the bar. My heart leapt; how I wished things could have been different, easier: I could have been a little younger or he a little older, and we could have shared a simple love between us. But he ignored me, bad luck for his soul.

He sat down at the bar, I sneaked in beside him and offered a glass of the house beer, slightly murky, with a lemony taste. It was as though the whole bar were conspiring with me: a young woman, slightly tipsy, bumped a waiter, who dropped his tray; a customer began to complain about the mess on his trousers while another shouted insults at no one in particular, all of which diverted Jacques Braise's attention. I poured the contents of my ring into his beer.

The effect was instantaneous. He slumped against me, shattering his glass. Before he could get too cold and arouse suspicion, I asked the barman to call a cab, and, joking together about the devastating powers of the house drink, we transported him to the back seat of the taxi.

The snow was still coming down like so many silent sorrows. The driver helped me carry him up to my bed. Jacques Braise was mine at last. Somewhat cold for the time being, but that was not important.

I undressed him. I was transfixed by his beauty, the harmony of his muscled limbs, the golden tuft of hair on his torso which, from now on, would crave only my caresses, his sex, which would rise for none but me. . . . I brought a crystal decanter to those too tender lips and eased the rim between his teeth; his soul, a supple mauve haze, poured into the bottle. I sealed the stopper with fresh wax and, to preserve it from the cold, I quickly buried the essence of Jacques Braise in my cellar, next to the oil furnace. Then I fed the corpse the antidote, a far easier concoction to prepare, consisting of salt, perfume, and one of my old teeth finely ground (I had preserved them all, just in case). Jacques Braise awoke, still glassy-eyed, from the dead, and the first thing he did was embrace me. My theft was a complete success; he was now in my power, my beloved object, my love zombie.

Naturally, he can no longer write his columns, so I dictate and he signs them. The magazine is delighted with his new style. As for my painting, I am now working exclusively on truncated perspectives.

Of course, at night, when he is lying in my arms, I can't really say he's mine body and soul. But in this *fin de siècle*, what more can one hope for?

COURAGE MAKES A FINE DAGGER

Dear Owner of Blue Locker 137,

Today, as winter loosened its grip on us just a bit and spring seems to have quieted the north wind, I decided to write to you. Because I don't know you. You've probably never even noticed me. We're both in the blue lockers section, which means you're also a sophomore, but we're not in the same class. You must be taking violin lessons, because every Tuesday and Thursday you leave school carrying a case. I've never seen anyone as quiet as you. Never. You remind me of the horizon at the edge of a wheat field, on TV. I've never been to the country. I'm writing this letter because I'd like to meet you. I'm writing this letter, but I may tear it up as soon as it's finished.

My name is Bruno, I'm fifteen. I'm going to be an astrophysicist and dedicate my life to studying the structure of the universe. The cosmos is so huge it shrinks all our problems, that's why. I know I'll have to study for a long time, but I'm not afraid; I'm used to working hard. In the morning, I deliver *La Presse*, I have fifty-nine subscribers. Evenings after class, I deliver groceries for a Portuguese grocery, *Soares and Sons, meat, cold beer and wines*, which comes in handy for our own shopping; and during summer vacations I work full-time washing dishes at Frites. Sunday, aside from my newspaper run, is my day off, except I have to do the week's cooking and cleaning. With the money I make, I'd like to buy myself a compact disc player or a mid-range telescope, but I can't. Right now it's eleven minutes after eleven o'clock, I just finished my homework, I can't see the moon from our basement window but I know it's in the first quarter, if I close my eyes I can see her shy smile.

I'd like to walk you to school in the mornings. If you agree. But lunch-time would really be the best time for us to be together. Together. Like twin stars. We could eat our sandwiches side by side in the cafeteria. We could sit in the no-smoking section, since you don't smoke either. To me, that would be like discovering a supernova! You'll laugh at me, but I'm dying to do two things: talk to you, and actually hear the radio waves from the nebulae. For the nebulae, I'd probably only have to go up to the observatory at Mount Mégantic on a Sunday, if I can get there. But you, these days you seem as far away as Alpha Centauri.

I figure you must be studying classical music, because of your violin. I'd really like it if, some time, you wouldn't mind playing a piece for me. Last year, in the Papineau subway station on the way to the planetarium with my class, I saw a real violinist for the first time. He had his case open at his feet for any money people might throw his way. This musician was concentrating very hard. And the melody! It was . . . it was sublime, not peaceful at all, the complete opposite, it was furious, with the rhythm of a raging heart! I had to stay with the group so I couldn't hang around and listen for as long as I would have liked. Pardiac, our physics teacher, told me it was Brahms. Afterwards, in the subway car, I closed my eyes to try to hold onto the echo of the music in my head, and, I don't know why, I saw the ocean beneath the constellations, waves attacking a stubborn cliff, the surf in wild rebellion in the air; if Pardiac hadn't been there, I would have missed our stop! As you can see, you could also talk to me about the sea, about which I know very little.

Did you hear about the Hubble space telescope the Americans put in orbit? That's the most exciting thing happening to me these days! It's an optical instrument smaller than the one on Mount Palomar, but its position in space will allow us to get images ten to fifteen times clearer than the ones we get with our telescopes on earth! We're getting closer to the stars! That's what convinced me to write to you at last.

Right now my mother is snoring. Good. Being a delivery boy, I'm very sensitive to atmospheric changes. Ride that bike, Bruno, through rain, wind, snow and slush, come on, Bruno, ride! Don't laugh, but when I was a kid, around ten, I made up a dog to help me out; he was invisible but huge. I named him Paradox. I had no idea what it meant, but I've always loved the sound of that word. Paradox pushes my bike from behind when I'm going up the hill on Sanguinet Street north of Ontario. He breathes on my neck when my worn-out jacket isn't warm enough against the drifting snow; sometimes, while I do my homework, he lies across my feet. Even though it's a bit childish, I still confide in him before I go to sleep. He's my only friend, except for Antonin. You must have noticed him, he's the school clown! Always falling all over himself, laughing for nothing. He likes to pretend he's dumb, but he reads a lot. Even more than I do. When I talked to him about you, he turned suddenly serious. Then he said: "If an ardent and lonely heart can attach itself so completely to a chimera, it is because she is real." Wow! That's from a letter Honoré de Balzac wrote to a stranger. It's amazing to think that a hundred years ago someone felt exactly the same thing I do! Anyway. Then

Antonin started to fall all over the lockers, shouting, "Bruno de Balzac! Bruno de Balzac!" What an ass. . . .

    Antonin's father was a journalist in Haiti. His mother and two sisters are staying with one of his aunts in New York, because they're too poor to live all together in Montreal. His father works here, in a slaughterhouse. It's bad enough spending your days in the company of animal corpses . . . but there's worse: before they carve up the cows, they have to skin them. Then they lay the skins in a room with no refrigeration or windows. Three weeks later, Antonin's father has to stretch out the skins and scrape the flesh off the insides. This is supposed to be relatively easy, since thousands and thousands of worms have already digested most of the meat. Easy!!? Apparently the worms are squirming all over the place and the smell is horrible. Some people in this world have it a lot worse than I do. I don't know why I'm writing you all this stuff about Antonin and his father. Maybe because, if I really told you about myself, I'd lose any hope of our ever holding hands. . . . Sometimes I wonder about your house, and your family. Have you lived in Montreal a long time? I really would like to get to know you. Sometimes I imagine the most awful things have happened to you. For example, I imagine that, to escape the rocket launchers, you and your family had to abandon Beirut and leave your house in ruins. Or your brothers were assassinated by Israeli soldiers, and you escaped from a refugee camp; you crossed Israel and all of Syria, to Turkey, months and months of walking across open country, having to hide at the slightest suspicious sound. Or maybe you come from the town of Halabjah in Iraq, and the only reason you didn't die of mustard-gas poisoning is that on that day, not wanting to bother anyone, you were practising your violin down in the cellar of your house? Maybe you were adopted by people here? I don't know you, but I'm sure you're very courageous. In this mean life, courage makes a fine dagger.

That's why I'm writing you. I think you'd understand me. Me and my mother . . . it's not easy to explain . . . I don't really have anyone to talk to. Since last Thursday I've been thinking about talking to the old punk lady, but I don't know. She's so strange, I'm not sure I can trust her. She moved into the area three years ago. She's my only subscriber who also gets *Le Devoir*, *Le Journal de Montréal* and *The Gazette*. Bizarre woman. I also deliver her groceries, every ten days. The punk lady has always got a different kid living with her. In the last thirty-five months, I've counted a total of five little girls. One girl was there for thirteen months, but another one lasted only six days. I think the punk lady is a foster home. Anyway. For the last two weeks she's had this little redhead, about seven years old, who cries absolutely all the time—skipping rope, on the swings in the park, she never stops! So last Thursday the two of them went to Soares's to buy some milk. They were playing a game together, arm in arm. The big one was describing the scenery: "I see a sheet of ice on the sidewalk, I see two birds in the sky . . . ," and the little one had her eyes shut. Her face was still shining from all the tears. Just as they walked past me, the punk lady said: "I see a fifteen-year-old boy with a face full of courage." I felt truly weird. I felt like crying, and then like telling her everything, this woman. But since I was loading empty bottles into the truck at the time, I kept my mouth shut.

I hope you like the card I've attached to this letter. The punk lady gave it to me, for Christmas. She'd slipped it into an envelope made of recycled paper, with my name on it, and she tied it to her doorknob with a bunch of different-coloured ribbons, so I could pick up my present at the same time as I was delivering her paper. She didn't write anything in the card. But on a separate sheet of pale green paper, she wrote this in purple ink:

> *Dear Bruno*
> *Under the snow, under the rock*
> *a diamond, always,*
> *waits to burn*
> Josse
> *P.S. Merry Christmas! You can always count on me*

    The poem is a bit corny, but I can't tell you how many times I've been carried away looking at the picture on that card! First of all I'm hypnotized by the background: all that turquoise blue, it must be the colour of the sky above the clouds, or, better still, the colour of the earth the astronauts see when they look down through their portholes. And in the upper right, the small child all wrapped up so you can't tell if he's sleeping or dead. And the warrior, down in the front to the left, with his bow and quiver: he's not really threatening, no, he looks kind of uncertain, or sad, as though the painter was saying something about the conditions of aboriginal peoples. That's one thing that makes me mad: when I think that, for over three hundred years, the whole of North America has been practising a kind of secret and vicious apartheid against Amerindians, I swear, it burns me up! I hope some day we give them back at least some of their land! What makes me even madder is that I can't do anything about it, nothing, just like with my mother, anyway. . . .

    Sorry, I got carried away there. I just went and got three sugar doughnuts from the fridge, I've liked them since I was a kid, it's the only treat I allow myself. I've

calmed down now. I never thought I could write such a long letter. I apologize. I feel like I'm unlocking my heart.
To get back to the painting. What I like best is the woman beside the Amerindian. She's so beautiful, with her dark garnet-red hat and her sweeping white dress! She looks like Mom did in the old days. On the back of the card, it says:

François Vincent
Paule series number 9 (the last)
oil on marouflage paper

Is Paule the wife of François Vincent? And what about "marouflage paper"? Do you know what that is? This picture's been my emergency exit so often when I've been depressed. Now it's yours. Next time I run into tough times, I'll try to invent myself a comet.

It's getting late. I should get to bed, or I'll be too tired tomorrow. I've just reread the beginning of my letter. I come off sounding too perfect. It's not true. Believe me. I'm going to tell you the truth: since I was nine, I've been a cheater and a thief. I cheat the government and I steal, but only from one person, my mother. It's not such a big thing, really: when the welfare and family allowance cheques come in the mail, I imitate my mother's signature and cash them. I'm the one who manages the family budget, so it's easier that way. That's not all. Sometimes, I feel like killing my mother. To put an end to her suffering. And to get a little peace for myself. Everything would be less complicated, and I'm perfectly capable of taking care of myself. My mother's been depressed for the last seven years. Every day I try to cheer her up. Every day I try to tell her a funny story. Or a happy story. I tell her one of Antonin's jokes. Or that they've invented a new drug for

AIDS. Or that, today, an old lady was singing while she planted flowers in the flowerbox on her balcony. It's no use. No use. I was eight years old the night it started, I'll never forget. Mom was still a nurse then. I was asleep but I got up when I heard her crying in the kitchen. She'd come back from her evening shift, her mouth all bloody and her clothes ripped. She walked me back to my room, told me not to worry, it was nothing. It wasn't nothing. Later, I figured out that maybe she'd been attacked, someone tried to rape her. She didn't go to the police, or maybe she did and I've forgotten. She never went back to work at the hospital. The first few months she stayed in bed, then she started drinking. She became confused and slovenly, and yet I never saw any alcohol in the house. A whole year later, on Mother's Day, I understood why. I decided to please her by washing everything: the floors, the walls, the windows. That's how I found out she'd replaced the contents of all the bottles of cleaning fluids with vodka. That Mother's Day was a disaster. . . . And then the landlord threatened to evict us because the rent was several months late. I was the one who found the dump, I mean the two-room apartment where we're living now. The last time my mother combed her hair and got dressed was to come and sign the lease. Even on July first that year, moving day, she wore her bathrobe. Luckily it was a Sunday, so Paulo, Mrs. Soares's nephew, was able to give us a hand with the grocery truck. Since then it's been downhill. Now she doesn't get out of bed, except to fetch her beer from the fridge when I'm at school. She orders it from Soares's and I bring it to her after the store closes. The damned vodka is too expensive, she only gets it on Christmas Eve. I can't see an end to it; even when I'm older, I'll still have to take care of her. Some mornings I get really down. I tell myself, if some poison got into her beer and my mother died without knowing it, it would be better for her. And for me. Then I feel guilty, it's awful. I want to disappear down some black hole, far away, far away. I'd like to be happy, just once in a while. I wish you were all there was in my heart. . . .

Please be kind enough not to breathe a word about this to anyone. You are the only two who know my secret now: Paradox and you.

But since the Berlin wall came down, it's crazy, I feel as though maybe, one day, Mom will pull out of it. . . .

THE LAST DAY FOR MILKSHAKES

Today, June twenty-third, at three-thirty, school ends. Through the open window you can hear the first-graders singing at the top of their lungs. Next to me, the twins, Odile and Béatrice, are happy. They're both my friends, but I like Odile better. My other friends, Laélia, Maria and Paula, the Portuguese girls, are also happy. Naturally, Patrick-the-pest is happy. Him I do not like. I don't like boys in general, but I hate Patrick. He's the one, at recess, who's always slamming the ball into my stomach as hard as he can. That just kills me. Zénaïde, our teacher, is wearing a dress with flowers so big they're deafening. No one in the class seems to be able to shut up: nobody has any discipline today. Even the sun. A big mouth full of teeth, that's the sun today. In other words, the entire universe is happy on account of summer holidays. Except me.

Seeing as it's the last day, we're allowed to do what we like. As long as we do it in silence. But silence has gone far away, to China, to Tiananmen Square. I saw it yesterday on TV. All cement, not a breath of wind. Silence is much too far away. So I'm writing. I like writing. I'll write anywhere. At my desk. On one of the computers in the classroom at lunch, whenever Zénaïde picks my name out of the hat. In my room, lying on my bed. On Josse's computer, when she's through for the day. Josse's computer has the most memory. In my class, I'm the one with the most memory. I may not know the answer to every question, but I never forget what's important. I'm very careful not to make mistakes when I write, because Josse says a mistake is like a greasy black stain on a brand-new sweater. Right now, I'm writing at my desk in my two-key diary. It was my only present for my first communion, April eleventh. Josse says she had trouble picking it out. But my diary is perfect: it's covered with pink camellias. It seems I have something in common with camellias, somehow. There's a lock. I always keep one tiny key to my diary in my left sock. I taped the second key, which is just as tiny, behind my bedside table. Tonight I must remember to hide it in my luggage. A second key is very important. Especially when they're so tiny.

Today I'm wearing my prettiest dress and matching socks. It's my first communion dress and it's dark blue and white, with stripes. There are forty-one stripes, I counted them. Twenty dark blue ones and twenty-one white, that's for good luck. Last night Josse ironed my dress using something that makes the material all stiff. Then she hung it in my room. It was as though there was an invisible little girl inside the dress. I wasn't afraid in bed. I was sad. I wanted to look at everything, so I would remember my room for ever. On the wall, there's a poem in a frame, a handwritten poem by Gilbert Langevin. I don't know who he is. I looked up the words I didn't understand, all by myself, in Josse's dictionary. Now I know the poem by heart. Even though I have an excellent memory, I'm going to recopy it here. Just in case.

SENSORIAL RESHAPING
To each body its weight of solitude
until that vermilion place where time turns
on its windy hinges

> where knives become
> daffodils and then
> to each desert
> a well of love

The same thing happens every time: I see oceans and oceans of hot sand, so hot that the horizon is completely hazed over, so hot that even the snakes and scorpions can't survive. And then suddenly I see a well, not very high, but with a shining pulley and a brand-new rope, and a roof. And I bend over the well, to see if there's any water. Yes! I turn the handle on the pulley and on the end of the rope I find an orange plastic bucket, full, actually running over with water. I drink the water and it tastes like chocolate ice-cream. And I ask Josse: "Would you like to smell the water?" I ask her that because Josse isn't allowed to eat chocolate, her doctor won't let her. Whenever I get some, she smells the wrapping, and she says it's almost as good; at least she gets an idea of the taste. She says that sometimes a scent can be precious.

But, getting back to my room, above the mirror there's that strange doll with the crooked smile, I chose her name myself: "Yesterday", because I like that word, "yesterday". I won't be able to take Yesterday with me tonight.

Before I came to Josse's, February twenty-seventh, my mother told me Josse had bought me. I didn't like that. It made me feel like an old black-and-white television all covered with dust. I waited until March twenty-third to ask Josse about it. We were walking on Saint-Denis Street, looking at the hats we could afford if we were rich, and I just said, kind of off-hand, " . . . So, Josse, did you really buy me?" She stopped us dead in our tracks and, forget the hats, she squatted down in front of me. I could see the tears clinging to the corners of her eyes as though they were afraid of falling into nothingness. She asked me to repeat what I'd said, because she hadn't quite heard. And then we started walking again. We didn't play the blind game at all that day. Josse told me about the last time people could buy other people. Legally and officially. That was a little more than a hundred years ago, in the United States, and it seems there was a war between those who were for slavery and those who were against it. These days there are still slaves, in the Dominican Republic and in South Africa, for example, but it's not legal or official, just awfully unjust. And then Josse ended up by telling me that, even if she became a millionaire, the richest woman in the whole wide world, even if she had the right to do it, there was no way she could ever buy me. Why? Because I'm worth too much, that's why. Me, Amélie Tremblay!

With my savings I bought a sheet of stamps and a whole bunch of pale purple envelopes. My mother is coming to get me tonight. She doesn't like Josse. She says Josse puts weird ideas in my head. I disagree. I love my mother. I love Josse too. It's not the same thing. My mother never helped me with my homework. My mother never really helped me at all. Maybe everything will be different now. During the holidays I won't have any homework. But I'll write lots of letters. Josse showed me where to print the address on the envelope, and where to put the return address, which is mine. She said I could write as many letters as I like, because a stamp costs almost nothing but a letter is as magnificent and precious as a piece of your heart.

This is the letter I'd like to write to Josse after the holidays:

Dear Josse,
We had a fine summer, not one rainy day. Mrs. Tran moved away on July first, but I got a chance to talk with her. She's expecting a child, she let me touch her belly and I felt the baby's foot move. I played out in the street all the time. How about you: have you finally finished your novel? I hope you found the ending. . . . My brother doesn't even notice me, I don't pay him any attention either, it's great. My mother is very very nice, she never screams any more. Did you read in the papers today that, in China, the students have finally won?!!
Your Amélie who thinks of you always
XXXXXXXX (kisses)

    Most of all, Josse has shown me that almost anything can become magnificent and precious. Before, there was nothing magnificent and precious in my life. Nothing. Anybody could just take my things and wreck them. Even my old doll, Dahlia, who's all torn up and dirty on account of my older brother, who messed around with her. My brother and my father, Dahlia and me, it's the same thing. Both wrecked. That just kills me. Josse told me that since Dahlia was with me when I was small, and since I told her all my secrets, that made Dahlia magnificent and precious. I've always wondered how Josse knew that. About the secrets and Dahlia, I mean.
    When it rains the blind game is even better, on account of the umbrella, which protects us both. I learned the game on March fourth. It's for when you go shopping every day with Josse. One of us is blind and the other one acts as her talking cane. The cane has to take the blind one's arm and warn her if there's a spot of ice or dog poo on the

sidewalk, or if people are coming. But even more important, the talking cane has to describe anything around that is really splendid to the blind one. There's always at least one really splendid thing. Always. Yesterday I saw two white butterflies. Together. Then the blind one can open her eyes.

Before, when I was small, I thought I wanted to become a cashier in a corner store, like Mrs. Tran down the street. Down the street from my mother's house, I mean. Once Mrs. Tran had a three-year-old child. He died in her arms, on a ship with too many people and not enough to eat. When I was young, Mrs. Tran was the saddest person on the face of the earth. Sadder than me, even. That's why I wanted to be a cashier in a corner store; because, according to her, it's a job that's comforting. But now I want to be an astronaut.

Josse has no boyfriends. Once she had one. But not now. She'd like to have one, maybe. We never talk about it. I prefer it that way.

But, getting back to my room, I have all kinds of books. Comic books for when I'm tired and other books for the rest of the time. Novels just for me. I'm going to leave them all in my room, for Josse's next almost-daughter. The Social Services have already told her the girl's name, Karina, and her age, eleven. Two years older than I am. The Social Services decide everything and there's no arguing with them. Take me, for example: I would have preferred to wait until after the holidays to go back to my mother's, because she'll be working during the day and I'll be all alone with my brother. I hope it won't rain too often during the summer. I feel safer in the street. But what if it rains. . . ? Josse and I tried to explain all that to the Social Services. But they say "the-family-fabric-has-been-reconstituted." But what colour is this fabric? Patrick-the-pest just threw a wad of paper down my neck. Next year I'll be in a new school. I just hope there's no Patrick-the-pest in every class on this earth. Or maybe you can't escape them, like nightmares? I'd like to give my father a whack on the head with a high-heeled shoe. A really sharp high heel. It's been a long time since I saw him. Since November fourteenth. I remember the date very well. Now he's in court. I hope he stays in court a long time, a very long time. The next time I meet him, I hope I'm an adult, a muscular adult, a karate black belt, that way I'll have the upper hand. Sometimes, when I can't sleep, Josse tells me to make up a story just for me, a story I'm happy in. This is my story: I'm walking in the street, I'm much older, I'm twenty-three, and I see my father coming down the street. He doesn't recognize me, because he hasn't seen me in a long time and I've grown a lot. But I recognize him, you bet! I give him a karate chop, and then I take off my high-heeled shoe and whack him. I told that story to Josse, on May twenty-first. The next day she went down to Saint-Laurent Street and found me a pair of plastic earrings shaped like high-heeled shoes. I thanked her, but I told her they were too small for my father's head. "Oh no," she said, "on the contrary." That really made me laugh.

Later I'll say goodbye to Odile, Béatrice, Laélia, Maria and Paula. I'd like to give something to Odile. I'm going to tell her my last secret. I'm going to tell her Josse is not my real mother. Only my almost-mother. On March second, when I came to school for the first time, everyone in the class thought she was my real mother. I was too shy to set them straight. Also, I was afraid they'd laugh

87

at me. Especially Patrick. That's how I became the only pupil with a mother who looks like a punk. Once, on March eighth, Josse picked me up after school. From behind the fence, a girl in sixth grade yelled at us: "Geez, is that your mother!?" Josse only squeezed my hand tight, so I didn't say anything either, except "Isn't she beautiful!" Afterwards, Josse told me about erosion. Erosion is a natural phenomenon that eats away at even the hardest rocks. She compared all secrets to a kind of erosion, an erosion of the soul. Even the kindest secrets, the smallest secrets, have this erosion effect. Except when you reveal them; then the effect becomes reversible, unlike real erosion. So later, once I've told my last secret to Odile, I'll be like a continent advancing into the ocean.

This morning Josse made me my favourite breakfast. She calls it "Tigress's Milk", but I think it's a milkshake with, aside from the milk, a banana, an egg, yogurt and wheat germ, which looks like powdered cardboard. But you can hardly taste the wheat germ, mostly it tastes like banana. I get to pick the colouring myself. Today I chose red and blue, which makes a greyish purple, a kind of nightfall purple, a melancholy purple. Melancholy, that's another pretty word, it sounds like a little bell ringing all by itself, far off in the distance. As usual, Josse sat at the kitchen table beside me and read the papers while she put on her nail polish. While her nails were drying, I put her cigarette in her mouth and lit it with the kitchen lighter, the pink one. The paper says twenty-seven students were executed by the Chinese government. For a moment Josse shut her eyes very tight, as tight as you have to shut the faucet in the bath, the one that leaks. That reminds me, tonight is garbage night, I have to get home quickly before she throws out the newspapers! I have to take down the names of the students in my two-key diary before I go. I have to make sure that at least I remember their names! But to get back to this morning, Josse also wanted to be happy, because of the summer holidays. I could tell she was trying hard, but it wasn't working. I heard her sigh long and deep while the blender was mixing the "Tigress's Milk". This morning, it was as though Josse and I were in there instead of the milkshake. In our hearts, I mean.

CELEBRATION OF GOOD WORKS

Until that day, my life had been dull, narrow and useless. And then one night, a call, inexplicable yet irresistible.... Expiation? Vocation? Revelation? I acquiesced: cashed in my pension fund, sold my furniture, tore up my passport, quit my job, my house, my few friends. I also killed my cat, but he was already very old. Finally, I gave my winter clothes away to the homeless: I wouldn't be needing them where I was going.

Other women, once upon a time, would have entombed themselves in a convent. I chose a cloister less boring than Toronto's, less foul-smelling than Paris's, and less dangerous than New York's. I resolved never to come up again into the open air. I didn't want to feel the cold anywhere but in my soul.

I entered into my cheerless monastery through its very nerve centre: the grey subway station at Berri-UQAM. On the way down, I left two suitcases of clean laundry in a locker in the bus station just above. To each his itinerary: some were heading for Florida or Chibougamau, I descended the concrete staircase. In my pockets I carried only a bank-machine card and an Opinel knife, emblems of my new order, or of the times.

I began my novitiate by taking inventory of the hundred kilometres and three million six hundred square metres of malls in my underground network; I took careful note of the hundreds of boutiques, doctor's and dentist's offices, beauty salons, shoemaker's stalls, banks, drugstores, dry cleaners, restaurants and galleries, the museum and the labyrinthine university, and all the movie houses, theatres, libraries, apartment and office complexes, train stations and hotels I could access without breaking my vow; but at the end of the first month, in a peach-coloured room in the Château Champlain Hotel above the Bonaventure station, I was visited by a horrible nightmare: transformed into a piece of cheese, I was being shredded to pieces through a giant grater. I woke up and immediately understood the message: this palatial comfort was a sacrilege; I must limit myself to a more rigorous asceticism.

I obeyed. The next day, sporting a platinum blonde wig, dark glasses and a spectacular miniskirt, I cornered a rather ugly sweeper during the off-peak hours in the Georges Vanier station and, forcing a voracious kiss on him, I snatched his set of keys before leaping onto a departing train. After that, I slept in broom closets, tucked in between four-wheeled cleaning buckets and malodorous mops. And meditated on this stinking life.

My days were measured by the rhythm of the crowds: in the early morning they were mostly immigrants, faces still misted over with dreams, followed closely by the usual combination of voluble and taciturn students; this was followed by swarms of fluttering saleswomen and secretaries bathed in clouds of perfumes; gradually the herd thinned out into the occasional broken old woman, strait-laced matron or unemployed worker, useless arms dangling at his sides, until the onslaught of the harassed five o'clock masses; in the evenings, I mingled with the youth of the upper classes in Place des Arts, joined the happy if thoughtless baseball fans beneath their crumbling stadium at Pie-IX, or shuttled over to Atwater station to knock around with the punks as they roughhoused their way towards a heavy-metal concert at the Forum. But it was the emptiness—a church-like emptiness which, at precise times, descended on each of the sixty-five stations—that attracted me. Enraptured me. Each of the stations, at its particular hour, deserted: a cathedral, a chapel, a sanctuary.... At approximately nine o'clock on a Tuesday evening, in Radisson station, I took my final vows.

It happened between the departure of two "ships", as the ticket agents like to call the suburban buses loaded with their human cargo. I had gone upstairs to the turnstiles; the attendant was gently nodding in a daydream. Standing at the foot of the stairs to the north side of Sherbrooke Street, I was contemplating an autumn sky clouded in mourning. To my right, a woman in a raincoat had just veered into the exit tunnel to Trianon Street. Suddenly I heard the muffled sounds of a struggle. I broke into a run. Opening my knife, without knowing why, and locking in the blade as I ran. In a corner where a map of the neighbourhood was displayed, the woman was pinned under a man who had clamped a hand on her mouth. I didn't stop to think: I hooked my left arm around the rapist's neck and plunged my Opinel in to the hilt. Below his left shoulder-blade. The aggressor reared back and released his prey. I dealt him several rapid thrusts: I wanted to strike the heart. I drew out the blade with a twist, to do more damage. The man's resistance grew increasingly weaker. Blood had begun to stain his black jacket. His victim recoiled in horror. I whispered to her to run: she took to her heels, straightening her clothes as she fled. Meanwhile the dying man collapsed against me. He was relatively short; I could see the discoloured tips of his crewcut. An ugly specimen. I watched with great interest as the cloud of death passed over his eyes. Afterwards, I laid the body carefully down onto the blue-tiled floor. I rolled my bloodied sweater under his head and placed his right forearm over his face. Two days later, the newspapers published the raincoat lady's description of her saviour, but this sketch of the Good Samaritan bore not the slightest resemblance to me. Until then I had been nameless. Now I was faceless. An anonymous sister. I remember the feeling of divine relief....

    I was called on to officiate again several weeks later, in the Villa Maria station, on a Monday afternoon shortly before four o'clock. Two subway trains had just passed in the station: seven minutes would now go by in silence. Seated on one of the two stairways at the disposal of disembarking passengers, I was giving thanks for this calm before the eruption of adolescents cavalcading out of the surrounding colleges. I heard someone scurrying along the opposite platform. The footsteps seemed to fade and then stop. Quiescence descended upon me. Five more minutes of beatitude. The memory of my past in the open air had grown so dim that it seemed to belong to someone else. Perhaps this vocation had been inscribed in my destiny long before my birth . . . perhaps from the beginning of time....

    A cry perforated the silence. Someone was trying to push a large woman onto the tracks. Watching her feeble attempts at self-defence, I could see that, in another two or three minutes, she would be reduced to a bloody porridge under the wheels of the lead car. I flew like the wind, grabbed the man by his hair and put out his eyes with perfect precision, driving the tip of my blade just far enough so as not to touch the brain. One second, a crazed stare; two seconds, dripping eyeballs; four seconds, I pulled the matron out of harm's way; eleven seconds, I was crossing the tracks without touching the high-tension wire; and by the time fifty-five seconds had elapsed, I was seated in a moving car, caressing the cheek of a baby in her stroller and singing praises to the beauty of innocence for her mother.

I was ordained in the Beaudry station, well before dawn on the first Sunday of January. (From November to March it was not possible to commune in the recently constructed sections of the subway, because the ventilation shafts there propel an absolutely glacial draft into the farthest reaches of the tunnels: I chose, therefore, to remain downtown.) On one of the built-in brown plastic seats, slumped against the two-tone tile wall, slept a dark, lovely stranger. I took up a post beside him to discourage anyone from robbing him in his sleep. An unnecessary precaution, no doubt; in the wake of the Christmas holidays, people were either hung over or holed up at home to escape the polar air. The relentless winter must have been torturing the country: a pool of melted snow had collected beneath the man's cowboy boots; the leather was encrusted with road salt—which the city dumps all over the streets at the slightest hint of snow. The expensive leather jacket may not have been his: the sleeves hung down over his fingers. Borrowed? Stolen? A moment of spontaneous generosity? I noted a peculiar trace of ether in the air around the attractive stranger. He woke with a start. A quick glance told him he had nothing to fear. What made him decide then to offer me his confession? Was it because he sensed that I had all the time in the world? He laid out his entire miserable life before me: the tragedy of a childhood cut short in the streets of Pointe Saint-Charles, the constant brawling, the prison stint for assault and battery, the infant daughter he was barred from seeing, the HIV diagnosis, and then the long ordeal of coke and crack—he showed me the rosary of bruises running down his tormented forearms—the two to three dozen tricks he was turning every day, and his last remaining wish: to overdose into eternal dreaming. That's when I offered to end it for him with a knife thrust to the heart, a more expeditious and less painful death than the slow agony to which he had been reduced. For the first time, I saw him smile. Before accepting. He unbuttoned his shirt. To pinpoint my target, I pressed my ear against the fading tattoo of a swallow on his chest. Softly I sang him an old lullaby until, still smiling, he slipped away.

    Since that day, I have been increasingly called upon to practise this, my arduous vocation. Almost every day now. . . . There seems to be no end to it. It makes you wonder whether life out there. . . .

IN THE WARMTH OF A PHRASE

She surfaces from the nightmare. Dawn is still a long way away, a long way. The luminous face of her alarm clock reads 4:37 a.m. She lingers a few seconds longer under the electric blanket, vainly hoping to store up the maximum amount of heat in her bones. How she envies those monarch butterflies rollicking beneath Mexican skies. She envies the polar bears buried snug in the cavernous darkness of their hibernation. She even envies those unborn children who lie coiled in the waters of their mothers' wombs.

But an unwritten story is calling impatiently for her; she must set the day in motion. She rummages under the sheets for her woollen socks, her heavy terrycloth bathrobe and her leather gloves with the fingers cut out. Stage one: without getting up, put on the socks, the gloves and the robe over her flannel pyjamas; stage two: jump into her slippers, run to the front of the apartment—turning on the lights as she goes—race down the stairs to the front door, grab the papers, climb the stairs four at a time, dive back under the electric blanket. She may just make it without taking a single breath, and so prevent the glacial air from entering her lungs. A short truce: now only the tip of her nose is exposed outside the blanket. But in the study in the front of the house, the unfinished tale frets; she can hear its lamentations. She sits up, shivering, grabs the remote control, zaps the television on to the weather channel—a minimum today of -23°C—and, combining frivolity with anguish, paints her nails while she reads the papers. She lights up her first cigarette, gratefully inhales the first puff: at last, a bit of heat in her throat. Stage four, the most difficult: to extricate herself definitively from the bed in order to select and prepare the four or five layers of woollens she will put on in fifteen minutes, after a boiling hot bath. Then moisturizer, eye shadow, mascara, eyeliner, demon red lipstick, perfume: poverty is no reason to feel like death or wear its complexion.

It's 5:31 a.m. She has downed a mouthful of milk and some vitamins. In her more than chilly study she sits down in front of the computer's cathodic glow. She covers her feet with a shawl; her cat once did a far better job at this, but she was obliged to part with it. She turns the heating-pad on behind her and sighs with pleasure, she dons her earphones—rock music pours into her head—she rubs her fingers, numb with cold, and begins reworking the half-completed pages. She works patiently, changing the tense of a verb here, an adjective there, altering the architecture of a relative clause, diving continuously into her well-worn dictionary. Eventually she forgets she's freezing. At 7:29 a watery sun checks in at her window. Each morning the same exhilaration: watching the night's retreat, the slow deployment of the dawn—with each morning's birth, she can feel her heart swell.

At 11:57 she prints out the few lines over which she has been slaving. She puts on her winter boots and her ratty old fur, and goes across the street to her neighbour's house for a bowl of piping hot soup. Now she can feel the ice jam in her veins begin to break up. Every noon, in her neighbour's kitchen, brings a new spring to thaw her blood.

Looking at her friend, she thinks of all those she has affectionately named her Private Arts Councils. She thinks of her mother, every Sunday evening, making a great show of disapproval as she slips her a choice morsel of chicken or beef; her mother paying for her newspaper subscriptions because she understands her thirst for fresh ink; her mother. She thinks of the journalist who shares the occasional complimentary tickets to a rock concert at the Forum, so she can feel fourteen thousand hearts pounding in unison. She thinks of the actor who, for thirteen years, has been taking her to the movies, where together in the dark they surrender themselves to those gigantic faces. She thinks: friendships are like the sowing of glowing embers.

(She doesn't know it yet, but a month from now her publisher will send her on a promotional tour across the province. In every hotel room, she'll turn the thermostats up all the way, shamelessly overheating, happily sweating and secretly thanking her publisher for these eleven days of false tropics. And in three days another friend, a friend of a friend who sits on a jury, will betray a slight confidence to tell her that she is about to be awarded a small grant by the province's Ministry of Cultural Affairs. And so, in February—that is, by the final days of February—her radiators will be blazing, she'll be writing in an incubator, in her very own Caribbean, having left behind, for this year, the polar land of so many painters and poets. Today, however, she knows nothing of all this.)

At one-thirty in the afternoon, she takes refuge in a bar three blocks from her house, where the waitress will let her nurse a single coffee through the afternoon. She scribbles the rest of her story in her notebook, imagines one or two twists, and gathers a few metaphors into the kindling which, in tomorrow's solitude, will burn for her.